S0-AXE-989

Disney
5-MINUTE STORIES
STARRING
DONALD

Disney PRESS
Los Angeles • New York

Collection Copyright © 2018 Disney Enterprises, Inc. All rights reserved.
"A Sure Cure for the Hiccups" written by Elle D. Risco. Copyright © 2015 Disney Enterprises, Inc.
"The Missing Recipe" based on the story written by Elle D. Risco. Copyright © 2014 Disney Enterprises, Inc.
"The Talent Show" written by Ellie O'Ryan. Copyright © 2018 Disney Enterprises, Inc.
"A Nice Day for a Sail" based on the story "Happy Sailing." Copyright © 2014 Disney Enterprises, Inc.
"Donald Takes a Trip" based on the story written by Kate Ritchey. Copyright © 2014 Disney Enterprises, Inc.

All illustrations by the Disney Storybook Art Team
Published by Disney Press, an imprint of Disney Book Group.
No part of this book may be reproduced or transmitted in any form or by any means, electronic or
mechanical, including photocopying, recording, or by any information storage and retrieval system,
without written permission from the publisher.

For information address Disney Press, 1200 Grand Central Avenue, Glendale, California 91201.
This special edition was printed for Kohl's Department Stores, Inc.
(for distribution on behalf of Kohl's Cares, LLC, its wholly owned subsidiary),
by Disney Press, an imprint of Disney Book Group, Los Angeles/New York.

Kohl's
Style Number 9781368043090
Factory Number 131635
06/18-08/18

Printed in the United States of America

First Hardcover Edition, August 2018
1 3 5 7 9 10 8 6 4 2
FAC-131635-18222
ISBN 978-1-368-04309-0

For more Disney Press fun, visit disneybooks.com

CONTENTS

A SURE CURE FOR THE HICCUPS

Mickey Mouse sighed. No matter what he did, he couldn't seem to stop hiccuping.

"What's wrong, Mickey?" Minnie asked, peering over the fence.

"Oh, hiya—*hic*—Minnie," Mickey said. "It's nothing. *Hic!* I just can't seem—*hic!*—to get rid of these hiccups!"

"Oh, my!" said Minnie. She thought and thought. Then she had an idea. "Daisy and I were about to go for a walk, but maybe we can help you instead."

"Help with what?" asked Daisy, walking up the garden path.

"Mickey has the hiccups!" said Minnie.

"Hic!" said Mickey.

Leading Mickey into the kitchen, Minnie poured him a glass of water.

"Close your eyes and take a tiny sip," she said. "Then count to five and take another sip."

Mickey closed his eyes and took a sip. Then he counted to five and took another sip.

"Did it work?" asked Daisy.

"I think it did!" said Mickey. "Thanks, Min—*hic!*"

"Hmmm . . ." said Minnie. "I think we need another idea!"

"It sounds like you need my tried-and-true hiccup cure!" said Daisy. "This may seem silly, but just do what I do."

Daisy twirled out Minnie's front door. Mickey did, too.

Daisy did two high kicks, tap-danced down the front walk, spun around once, and took a bow.

Mickey started to do the same, but halfway through—*"Hic!"*

"Maybe Donald knows a good cure for the hiccups," said Minnie. "Let's go ask him!"

The three friends set out to find Donald. But Minnie
and Daisy were much faster than Mickey. When he arrived at
Donald's house, they were waiting by the front door.

"Where's Donald?" Mickey asked.

Before Minnie could answer, Donald jumped out at Mickey.

"Boo!" he shouted.

"Aaah!" Mickey cried.

"Sorry, Mickey," Donald said. "Minnie said you had the hiccups. I thought maybe I could scare them away. Did it work?"

But Mickey just hiccuped again.

Mickey tried everything he could think of to get rid of his hiccups. He skipped rope and sang, "M, my name is Mickey—*hic*—I have a friend named Minnie—*hic*—and I like mints! *Hic! Hic!*"

He stood on his head while saying the alphabet backward. *"Hic!"*

He held his nose and whistled a tune while hopping on one foot. *"Hic!"*

Nothing worked!

Mickey sat down in Donald's hammock and moped. He was starting to feel like he would never get rid of his hiccups.

"It's no use," he told his friends. "I think they're—*hic*—here to stay."

Minnie led Daisy and Donald to the side of the yard. "I have one last idea," she told them.

The three friends whispered to one another for several minutes. Finally, Donald rushed inside and returned with a large sack.

"We've got it, Mickey," Donald said. "The cure for your hiccups is right in here!"

Donald handed the sack to Minnie, who pulled out some blocks. Concentrating hard, she balanced three of them on her nose.

Next, Daisy and Donald pulled two toy rings out of the sack. They hung one on each of Minnie's arms, and she began to twirl them.

"Okay, Mickey!" Minnie said. "It's your turn."

Mickey wanted to try, but all he could do was laugh.

"I'm sorry, Minnie," he said between giggles. "You just look
so . . . silly!"

When Mickey finally stopped laughing, he realized
something. His hiccups were gone!

His friends waited and waited, but not another hiccup came.

"I did it!" shouted Minnie. "I cured Mickey!"

"You sure did, Minnie," said Mickey. "I guess laughter really
is the best medicine . . . for hiccups!"

THE MISSING RECIPE

Mickey Mouse was relaxing in his living room when the doorbell rang. Mickey opened the door. Outside was a very panicked Minnie.

"Gee, what's wrong, Minnie?" Mickey asked.

"Oh, Mickey, it's awful," said Minnie. "Today is the annual Bake-Off, and I can't find my cinnamon swirl cake recipe!"

Just then, Pluto ran up the driveway. He dropped a rolled-up paper at Mickey's feet and began to bark.

"Thanks, Pluto," Mickey said. "But right now we have to help Minnie. Come on!"

Back at Minnie's house, Mickey searched the kitchen.
But the recipe was nowhere to be found.

"It was on the counter this morning," Minnie said. "I don't
know what could have happened!"

Suddenly, Mickey noticed a postcard on the floor. "What's this?" he asked.

Minnie giggled. "Donald came over this morning to show me his postcard collection. He was so excited to show me his newest ones that he dropped the whole stack on the counter. That one must have fallen on the floor."

That gave Mickey an idea. "Maybe Donald accidentally picked up your recipe with his other postcards. Let's go ask him!"

Mickey, Minnie, and Pluto headed over to Donald's house.
But when they got there, they found Donald angrily pacing his
living room.

"What's wrong, Donald?" Minnie asked.

"It's my new postcards! They're missing!"

Donald showed Mickey and Minnie his postcard collection. "See? Five of them are missing!"

"I'm missing my cinnamon swirl cake recipe, too!" said Minnie.

"We were wondering if you might have picked it up by accident when you were at Minnie's this morning," Mickey said.

As Donald stared sadly at his postcard collection, Pluto dropped the rolled-up paper on the table. But Donald was too upset to notice.

"Where was the last place you saw your postcards?" Mickey asked.

Donald thought. "I was flipping through them when I came back from Minnie's house," he said. "I came through the door . . . and tripped over Huey! The boys were working on a collage in the hallway!"

"Oh, my!" said Minnie. "You don't think they accidentally used some postcards in their collage, do you?"

Pluto barked and dropped the paper at Minnie's feet.

"Thanks, Pluto," said Minnie. "But we have to solve this mystery!"

And with that, Minnie, Mickey, Donald, and Pluto went to wait for the boys at the bus stop.

"Boys," Donald said when his nephews got off the school bus, "did you use my postcards in your collage?"

Donald's nephews blushed. "Those were yours, Uncle Donald?" Huey asked.

"We thought they were pieces of junk mail," Dewey said.

"Junk mail!" cried Donald angrily.

"Now, now," said Minnie calmly. "It was just an accident, Donald." Then she turned to Huey, Dewey, and Louie. "Where is the collage now?" she asked the boys.

Louie shrugged. "It's the strangest thing," he said. "I rolled it up and put it in my backpack this morning."

"But when we got on the bus, it was gone," Dewey said.

"It must have fallen out somewhere between Donald's house and the bus stop," Minnie said.

The group searched everywhere, from the bus stop all the way back to Donald's house. They even checked Mickey's and Minnie's yards. But they couldn't find the collage anywhere.

Pluto whined and dropped his rolled-up paper at Huey's feet.

"Hey!" Huey shouted, looking down. "This is it! Pluto had it all along!"

"We must have dropped it in Mickey's yard after all," said Dewey.

"And Pluto found it!" said Louie.

The boys unrolled the paper and showed off their collage, complete with Donald's postcards and Minnie's missing recipe!

Minnie giggled. "You were trying to help us all along, Pluto!" she said. "I'm going straight home to bake two cinnamon swirl cakes. One for the contest and one for you!"

And that is just what she did!

THE TALENT SHOW

Mickey Mouse sighed as he looked out the window. It was pouring outside.

"Sorry, gang," he said. "It doesn't look like we'll be able to go for a hike today after all!"

"Now what are we going to do?" Donald asked.

"I have an idea!" Minnie said. "Let's put on a talent show. We can have it right here."

"And we can invite all our friends!" added Mickey.

Donald had a great idea for an act—but he couldn't do it alone.

"Hey, Pluto! Want to be in my act?" he asked.

Pluto barked happily.

"Great!" Donald replied. He dashed to the kitchen. A few minutes later he came back carrying a large bowl of fruit.

Everyone was curious about Donald's props, but he didn't want to ruin the surprise. "Come on, Pluto!" he said. "Let's go practice in the attic."

Donald waited until they were all alone to tell Pluto about his big idea. "We're going to have the best act in the talent show!" he exclaimed. "I'm going to juggle this fruit. Then I'll throw it to you one piece at a time so you can balance it on your nose."

Donald grabbed an apple, a peach, and a pear. "Watch this!" he said.

Donald tossed the fruit into the air and started to juggle. Pluto was so impressed that he sat back and barked his approval.

"Good! You sit—just like that!" Donald told Pluto. "Now I'll throw the fruit over . . . one at a time. Okay? One . . . two . . . *three*!"

Just as Donald tossed the peach to Pluto, the attic door creaked open.

Pluto spun around to see who was there. The peach sailed past his head and landed on the floor with a juicy *splat*!

"I just wanted to see if you'd like to help invite our friends to the talent show," Daisy said, holding up a phone.

"Can't you see we're practicing?" Donald snapped. Then he closed the door—right in Daisy's face.

Donald picked up the smashed peach. "Yuck!" he said. "I can't juggle with this!"

Donald plucked a plum from the fruit bowl and started juggling again. The fruits went *whoosh—whoosh—whoosh* through the air.

This time, when Donald tossed the plum into the air, Pluto was ready. He caught it on his nose!

"Great job!" Donald cheered. "Okay, here comes the pear. . . ."

Knock-knock-knock!

Pluto and Donald jumped!

The plum rolled off Pluto's nose, and Donald dropped the pear and the apple accidentally. All the fruit went *splat*!

"Hi there, Donald! Howdy, Pluto! Wow, it looks like you're working really hard!" Mickey said. "I can't wait to—"

"What do you want?" Donald grumbled.

"We're almost ready to go on," Mickey replied. "I was wondering if you'd like to help decorate the set!"

"We don't have time for that!" Donald said. "Can't you see we're practicing?"

"Oh," Mickey said. "Sorry to bother you."

Donald took a deep breath and picked up another apple. "It's almost time for the show," he said, "and we *still* haven't practiced all the way through!"

Pluto looked worried.

"It's okay, Pluto," Donald continued. "I'm good at juggling things, and *you're* good at catching things. I'm sure it will be—"

Just then, Minnie poked her head into the attic. "Does anybody need help with their costumes?" she asked.

"No!" Donald hollered. "What we need is *practice*—and no more interruptions!"

"I'm sorry," Minnie replied. "But Mickey also asked me to give you a message. The show is about to start!"

Donald peeked out the attic window. Sure enough, he could see Huey, Dewey, and Louie dodging raindrops as they hurried to the house.

"Good luck with your last practice," Minnie said in a small voice before she slipped out the door.

Donald glanced at the fruit bowl. It had looked so full before, but now there were only a prickly pineapple, a watermelon, and a bunch of bananas left. There was barely enough fruit to juggle in the show, let alone to practice with.

When they went downstairs, Donald and Pluto could see how hard everyone had worked to get ready for the talent show. Donald wondered how they'd had time to practice their own acts.

"I'm sorry," Donald said. "I should've helped everybody get ready—instead of yelling at you for interrupting my rehearsal."

Mickey smiled and stepped in front of the audience. "Welcome, friends, to the Rainy Day Talent Show!" he announced.

Donald watched as his friends shared their acts. First Mickey performed an amazing magic trick. Then Minnie did a special dance. Next Daisy played a song on her harmonica.

"You're up!" Mickey told Donald and Pluto. "Break a leg!"

Donald and Pluto walked to the center of the stage. As Pluto sat back on his haunches, Donald grabbed the bunch of bananas.

But Donald had never juggled with a bunch of bananas before! The bananas flew across the room, making the whole audience laugh.

Donald's cheeks turned pink as he grabbed the pineapple and tossed it into the air. "Ouch—oof—ow—ugh!" Donald exclaimed as he tried to juggle it. He glanced at Pluto, who shook his head and hid under his paws.

Soon only the watermelon was left. When Pluto saw Donald reach for it, he hid under the couch!

The audience howled with laughter.

Too embarrassed and upset to face his friends, Donald rushed off the stage.

Pluto nuzzled his hand. A few minutes later, Mickey, Minnie, and Daisy joined them.

"What's wrong, Donald?" Daisy asked.

Donald stared at her in amazement. "What's *wrong*?" he said.

"Everything! My act was a disaster! It made everyone laugh and turned me into a big joke!"

"Actually," Mickey said, "you and Pluto were the stars of the show!"

"That's right," Minnie agreed. "We wanted to entertain our friends, and you did. Everyone's having a great time!"

"In fact, I can still hear them clapping," Mickey added.

Donald couldn't believe it, but Mickey was right. Everyone *was* clapping!

"You'd better get out there and give them an encore," Mickey told him.

"I don't have enough fruit," Donald said. "Pineapples and watermelons were not made for juggling!"

"How about you juggle balls instead?" Daisy suggested.

"And we'll save the fruit for fruit salad!" Minnie said, giggling.

A NICE DAY
FOR A SAIL

Mickey and Minnie were relaxing in the park when Huey,
Dewey, and Louie appeared in their sailboat. "Hiya, Mickey. Hiya,
Minnie," the boys said. "Nice day for sailing, isn't it?" Mickey and
Minnie nodded and waved to the boys as they sailed away.

Suddenly, Mickey had an idea. "Say, Minnie," he said, "it *is* a nice day for sailing." Mickey pointed to a boat tied up by the water. "How about we go for a ride, too?"

"I would love to," Minnie said with a smile. "A nice, easy ride sounds like the perfect way to spend the day."

Mickey and Minnie climbed into the boat and began to row away from shore. They had not gone far when a squirrel leaped into the boat with them! Startled, Mickey and Minnie jumped back . . . and landed right in the water.

Mickey and Minnie climbed back into the boat and rowed
to shore.

"How about a little lunch while we dry off?" Mickey
suggested.

Minnie thought that was a wonderful idea. Soon the two
were relaxing in the sun with hot dogs.

As they were enjoying their lunch, Pluto came running by. Seeing the hot dogs, he decided he wanted one, too. He jumped into Mickey's lap and tried to grab the food.

"Stop it, boy!" cried Mickey.

"Pluto," said Minnie, "if you want a hot dog, we can get you one of your own."

But it was too late. Pluto knocked Mickey and Minnie right into the water.

Donald Duck was nearby in his speedboat and saw what
happened. He helped Mickey and Minnie into his boat. "Why
don't you ride with me for a while?" he said. "You can take it
easy and let the engine do the work."

Mickey and Minnie sat back and relaxed, listening to the happy *putt-putt* of the engine. They had just reached the middle of the lake when the boat's engine suddenly stopped.

"What do we do now?" Minnie asked.

"I have an idea," Donald said. He took off his hat and started to paddle with it.

Mickey and Minnie did the same. Huffing and puffing, they made their way back to shore.

Back on shore, Huey, Dewey, and Louie had finished their sail. "Do you want to borrow our boat?" Huey asked Minnie. "There's a nice wind today."

Minnie thought. "I guess we could *try* sailing one more time," she said.

And so Mickey and Minnie set off in the boys' boat. But after a few minutes, the wind stopped blowing.

"Oh, no!" Mickey groaned. "We're stranded again!"

Mickey and Minnie tried to paddle with their hands, but it was no use. They just kept going in circles. "What are we going to do now?" asked Minnie.

Suddenly, Mickey looked up. Goofy and Donald were coming toward them in rowboats.

"We thought you might need some help," said Donald.

"Hyuck," said Goofy. "How about a tow to shore?"

As the sun began to set over the peaceful lake, Mickey and Minnie sat back and smiled. They had finally gotten their nice, easy boat ride!

DONALD TAKES A TRIP

Mickey Mouse was relaxing in his living room when, suddenly, the doorbell rang. Mickey opened the door to find a very upset-looking Donald.

"What's wrong, Donald?" Mickey asked.

Donald sighed. "It's too hot at my house. Can I stay with you for the day?"

Mickey happily invited Donald inside. And then Minnie . . .
and Goofy . . . and Daisy! The friends were just deciding what to
do with their day when—*pop!* Mickey's air conditioner broke!

"Maybe there will be a breeze outside," said Minnie.

But there was no breeze. Just nice, cool lemonade from
Mickey's refrigerator.

"Gosh! Those sprinklers look nice and cool!" said Goofy, pointing down at Mickey's lawn.

Donald nodded. "But there isn't enough water coming out of them to keep us cool!" he said.

"It's too bad the town pool doesn't open until next week," said Mickey.

As Minnie watched her friends looking at the sprinklers, she suddenly had an idea.

Minnie jumped out of her chair. "I've got it!" she shouted.
"Let's go to the lake! There's always a breeze there, and there's
so much to do!"

"What a great idea!" said Mickey.

"It *is* the perfect day for a swim," Daisy added.

Minnie and her friends raced home to pack. Minnie quickly threw her bathing suit, a towel, and a beach ball into her bag. Then she headed back to Mickey's house.

In no time, the friends were on their way. As they drove, they sang songs and played games. They were so excited for their day at the lake!

By the time the friends arrived, they had cooled off.

"What should we do first?" Minnie asked.

Everyone had a different idea. Daisy wanted to play basketball. Mickey and Pluto wanted to play Frisbee. And Donald wanted to go fishing!

Before anyone could stop him, Donald raced off toward a little boat docked beside the water.

Donald was already jumping into the boat when Minnie called out to him. "Wait up, Donald," she said. "I don't think we can all fit in the boat. Let's do something together!"

"But the water looks so nice!" said Donald.

"Why don't we go for a swim?" said Minnie. "We can *all* do that!"

Donald really wanted to go fishing, but finally he agreed.

After all, they *had* come to the lake to go swimming.

So the friends put away their toys and jumped into the water. . . .

"Aah," said Mickey. The water felt nice on the very hot day.

Donald leaned back and closed his eyes. "You were right, Minnie. This was a good idea!"

Minnie smiled to herself. She was glad she and her friends had found a way to cool off.

"I could stay in this water all day!" Daisy said.

And that is just what they did.

As the sun set and the day started to get cooler, Minnie and her friends got out of the water.

"I guess it's time to go home," Daisy said with a sigh.

But Minnie had one last surprise for her friends . . . s'mores!

"Gee, Minnie," said Mickey as they roasted marshmallows over a campfire, "you really do know how to plan the perfect day!"

Finally, it really was time to leave. Minnie and her friends packed their bags and got into the car.

"That was so much fun!" said Donald as they drove home. "Let's do it again tomorrow!"